Going for Gold

by
Anne Schraff

Perfection Learning® Corporation
Logan, Iowa 51546

Editor: Paula J. Reece
Cover Illustration: Doug Knutson
Cover Design: Deborah Lea Bell
Michael A. Aspengren

For information, contact
Perfection Learning® Corporation
1000 North Second Avenue, P.O. Box 500
Logan, Iowa 51546-0500.
Tel: 1-800-831-4190 • Fax: 1-712-644-2392
Paperback ISBN 0-7891-5362-9
Cover Craft® ISBN 0-7807-9737-x
Printed in the U.S.A.
4 5 6 PP 06 05 04

1

Keely Wayne sat on the floor of the gym. She stretched her legs first. Then her back, neck, and arms. As she limbered up, Keely tried to think back to a time when gymnastics wasn't a part of her life. She couldn't.

Keely had started with dance class when she was four. Then when she was eight, some of the girls had switched to gymnastics. Keely had decided to give it a try too.

After her first class, Keely's father had appeared in the doorway of her bedroom. Keely was bubbling with excitement.

"You had fun today, huh?" Keely's dad had asked with a pleased smile on his face.

"Oh, yeah," Keely had said. She was still wearing her purple leotard. "Miss Lundquist said the dance lessons I've taken will really help me when I compete in gymnastics. I'll look more graceful."

After only a month of lessons, Keely's instructor had recognized her talent. Keely worked with Miss Lundquist until she was 11. By then, Keely had advanced through level 7.

Keely understood how the gymnastics system was divided into levels. Levels 1–10 were followed by the elite levels, National Elite and International Elite. A gymnast moved through the levels by performance testing at the lower levels and scoring high in meets at the higher levels.

After Keely had passed level 7, Miss Lundquist had called in Keely's parents. Miss Lundquist had told them that she could no longer give Keely the advanced instruction she needed. And she recommended Keely enroll with Wassily Karpov. He was the best coach in the area. His team had brought home silver and bronze in the last Olympics.

Keely had been excited at the prospect of becoming a "real" gymnast, like all those girls she had been reading about and watching for years. But her dad had been even more excited. Keely remembered the look on his face when he had realized that Keely had "made it to the big time."

Keely's dad was a tall, handsome man. He had a high-level position as a chemist in an international company, and he was only 39. Plus he was the only African American in such a prestigious position with the company. Keely was very proud of her father.

But she was also a little afraid of him. She worried that she might fall short of her father's high aspirations for her.

Keely remembered when her dad's intensity and pressure had started to heat up. It was not long after Keely had started at Wassily's gym.

"Did Wassily say anything about your figure, Keely?" her dad had asked that day.

Kelly had stiffened. It was the first time her dad had ever talked about her body. "What do you mean, Dad?" she asked.

"You've got to watch your weight, Keely," her dad had said. His critical eye fixed on the granola bar in Keely's hand. "Stay away from those munchies if you want a gymnast's figure. You must ask yourself if you want to go for the gold at the next Olympics, or if you want to be a chubby little nobody in the world of gymnastics."

Keely was 11 years old when that had happened. She was now 14. She was a little over 5 feet tall and weighed 100 pounds.

A lot had happened since she started training with Wassily. She had advanced through level 10 and reached the elite stage. The road to this level included hours of practice each day and meets every weekend. She was now a member of a gymnastic team training hard for the Olympic Trials which were less than two years away.

Keely trained for four hours every day after school. She enjoyed the floor exercises, the uneven bars, the balance beam, and the vault. But she was terrified of gaining weight and losing her chance for the gold.

On this day, Keely and her teammate Adrienne Thorn were supposed to work on floor exercises under Coach Wassily's guidance.

Keely went first.

"Show me your flic-flac," said Wassily.

Keely jumped backwards with both feet and landed on her hands. Then she sprang and landed on her feet. This move was also called a back handspring.

"Keep your legs together," barked Wassily. "Now give me a salto followed by a full-in."

Keely stood at the edge of the tumbling mat. She took a deep breath and ran toward the opposite edge. She quickly flipped in the air. Her feet came up over her head, and her body rotated around the axis of her waist. Then she went right into a double somersault with a full twist in the first somersault.

Keely stood catching her breath as Wassily yelled, "You are sloppy! Watch Adrienne!"

Keely watched as Addy performed a full-in followed by a triple twist. Even though she was supposed to be noticing Addy's technique, Keely couldn't help but notice Addy's thighs. Keely thought about how slender and pretty they looked. Keely hated the way *her* thighs looked.

Why do I have such fat, ugly thighs? Keely thought. *When we go to the Trials, that's all the judges will notice!*

After practice, Keely and Addy sat by the outside door and waited for their parents to pick them up. Keely couldn't stop thinking about her fat legs. So she asked Addy, "How do you keep so nice and thin?"

Addy laughed and said, "You're skinnier than I am!"

"No, I'm not," Keely groaned. "You look so great in that black leotard. I feel so fat and lumpy. Even Wassily was bugging me yesterday about my weight. He called me a *butterball*."

"Oh, Keely, you know how Wassily likes to exaggerate to motivate us," Addy said. "You've got great thighs."

"I skip meals a lot. And I chew gum when I get hungry instead of snacking. But still, I can't lose a pound!" Keely said.

"If I diet too much, I get weak," Addy said. "Then I don't have the strength it takes to perform my stunts."

"Wassily said that for my height I'd be perfect if I weighed 95 pounds," Keely said. "That's five pounds less than I weigh now. Why is it so hard to lose five measly pounds?"

Another girl, Liza Duncan, joined them. Keely really envied her. Liza was strong, graceful, and *small.* Keely bet that Liza, who was Keely's height, weighed no more than 95 pounds.

"I heard you guys talking," Liza said. "It's easy to lose weight."

"Easy?" Keely cried. "Two days last week I ate nothing but bouillon cubes and diet gelatin desserts, and I didn't lose a single pound!"

Liza massaged her beautiful, slim legs and said, "I eat anything I want. I eat chocolate cake and ice cream and thick, juicy steaks if I want. Even cheesecake!"

Keely stared at Liza in disbelief. "You must have some incredible metabolism that just eats up calories, Liza. You are so lucky!" Keely said. "I'm just like my mom. Everything we eat ends up on our legs and stomachs. Mom has thunder thighs. It's like a curse, a genetic curse."

"It's got nothing to do with genetics," Liza said. "You just eat all you want. Then you stick your finger down your throat, and *voila*, it's gone."

"You mean throw up all the time?" Keely asked. "Oh, that's disgusting!"

Liza shrugged. "Not as disgusting as fat thighs." She walked over to the bars and leaned on them, moving her slim legs sideways and backwards.

Keely looked at Addy. "You don't do that, do you?" she asked.

Addy looked nervous for a minute. Then she said, "Sometimes I use a lot of . . . you know . . . laxatives, and that helps me keep my weight down. But mostly I exercise. I run miles and miles. If you want to lose weight and keep it off, you've got to run. Keep moving all the time."

Keely's mother pulled up in the van. Keely said good-bye to her friends and ran out to catch her ride.

As she sat down in the passenger seat, Keely stared critically at her mother's figure. Her mom was wearing a T-shirt and shorts. She really looks terrible, Keely thought. Her mom was 5 foot 4 and weighed at least 135. Keely couldn't imagine why her mother wore shorts when she was so chubby.

"How was your day, Keely?" her mom asked breezily.

"Okay," Keely said. "Wassily said that I'm improving every day. He said if I do well at the invitational in a few weeks, then maybe I can go on tour."

Keely's mom said, "Don't forget that you're only a freshman, honey. You should be thinking about school. You've got three more years after this year."

"Wassily said that the really good gymnasts often drop regular school and get their education from correspondence school. That's so they have more time to practice in the gym," Keely said. Even as she said the words, she felt sad. Keely loved gymnastics. But she liked going to West Bluff High School too. She'd already made some nice friends, including a dark-eyed boy named Julio Healey.

"You know, honey," Keely's mom said, "most girls who take gymnastics never get to the Olympics. There's really just a minuscule chance you'll make it. I hate to see you throw everything else away and focus entirely on gymnastics."

"But, Mom, what if I *am* good enough to win a gold medal?" Keely said. "Imagine what a thrill that would be. And everybody would be so proud of me. Especially Dad."

"Your father is proud of you right now," Mrs. Wayne said.

"Yeah," Keely said. But deep in her heart she knew that her dad was much prouder of her 18-year-old brother, Mac. Mac was already a sophomore at the University of Southern California. He was a star on the Trojan football team, and he was majoring in biology. Keely made good grades, but Mac was a straight-A student. Keely's dad just seemed more impressed by Mac.

When Keely and her mom got home, Keely remembered that she had a history test the next day. But she really didn't have time to study for it. She thought about what Addy had said about running. The neighborhood where Keely lived was hilly. She thought it would be good for working off weight. So Keely ate half an apple and slipped into her jogging clothes.

"Where are you going?" Keely's mom asked. "You just got home."

"I just feel like a little run, Mom. Wassily said running is really good for developing strength. You need strength and speed in gymnastics," Keely said.

"Well, don't be gone too long," her mom said. "Dinner will be ready soon, and I'm making your favorite—sweet-and-sour stuffed pork chops. You know how you like them!"

"Okay, Mom," Keely said, running down the walk and then along the street. She thought of the sweet-and-sour pork chops. Her mom was the best cook of anybody she knew. But those pork chops must have a billion calories, Keely thought glumly. But, oh, they were so good! Cornbread stuffing, brown sugar, crushed pineapple . . .

It was growing darker earlier and earlier. By the time Keely reached the end of the street, it was almost completely dark. A silver moon rolled in the sky, like a farmer's scythe.

"Hey, Keely," a familiar voice rang out.

Keely turned to see Julio Healey driving alongside her.

"What are you doing over here?" she asked.

"Visiting my grandparents," Julio said. Julio lived in a more modest end of town about three miles away. "What are you doing running around in the dark?"

Keely smiled at Julio. He had just turned 16, and he had a little old Chevy pickup that he and his grandfather had restored together. Julio had a smile brighter than a hundred candles shining in a room.

"I'm trying to run off some weight," Keely said.

"No way!" Julio said. "Are you serious?"

"Yeah. Wassily, my coach, said it'd be good if I lost about five pounds," Keely said.

"Keely, you're just right! You could add a few pounds and look even better. This Wassily guy must be crazy," Julio said.

Keely was flattered that Julio was talking like that. But he just didn't understand the world of gymnastics.

"If I work hard enough on my gymnastics, I might go on tour," Keely said. "I've got to look my best. I can't have ugly, fat thighs. The judges are supposed to critique the girls on their performances, but they can't help but look at the girls too. A slender, pretty girl has a better chance than some chunky girl."

"You're not chunky, Keely. You never could be," Julio said.

"Oh, yeah, I could," Keely said. "If I don't watch my weight, I could get fat like my mom."

"What are you talking about?" Julio asked. "Your mom's not fat."

"I just wince when I see Mom in shorts," Keely said. "And I'm scared of getting like that."

Julio shook his head. "Well, anyway, I don't like you running around these streets in the dark, Keely."

"This is a nice neighborhood. I'm safe enough," Keely said.

Keely's father's job made it possible for the Waynes to live in a rather affluent neighborhood. Many of the other students at West Bluff lived in a rougher area. Keely's dad always reminded the family of how lucky they were.

"That's why we've got to use every single opportunity to get ahead," Keely's dad would often say. "That's what life is all about—grasping opportunity. I could have settled for some second-rate job. But I worked hard and got a scholarship. And now look where we are. Life is happening right now, and if we don't make the most of every chance, we're losers. We don't get second chances."

Julio followed Keely in his car until she got home.

As Keely came up the walk in a run, her dad grinned. "Keely, you're running! That's great," he said. He was setting out the garbage on the curb.

"Yeah," Keely said. "It's good for a gymnast to run. Develops more strength in your legs for the vaults."

Keely's dad continued to grin. "Slims down those fat little legs too, Keely," he said. "I've noticed you've been packing it in at the table." Then he winked.

A cold chill went down Keely's spine.

2

Keely felt panic grip her. If even her dad noticed her fat thighs, she *must* have gained weight. Keely rushed to the bathroom and stepped on the scale. She was almost afraid to read the numbers.

Keely glanced down. Ninety-nine pounds! Oh, thank goodness, she thought. I didn't gain any weight, and I even lost a pound!

The fragrance of her mom's stuffed pork chops filled the house. Keely was so hungry. Her mouth watered at the thought of the sweet-and-sour pork chops.

But I shouldn't eat them, Keely told herself. I should just eat a lettuce and tomato salad with low-calorie dressing . . .

"Come on, sweetie," her mom called from the dining room. "Dinner's ready."

Keely joined her parents at the table. The pork chops looked so heavenly. They were golden brown with the savory stuffing spilling out. They sat on a bed of little roasted onions and green and yellow pepper strips.

Keely's dad had a sleek, hard body. He had wrestled in college. He still played a mean game of volleyball. He was the ideal weight for a man his age.

"Now, don't eat too much, babe," her dad said when Keely sat down.

"She needs to eat," said her mom. But one stern look from her husband hushed Keely's mom. Mr. Wayne didn't like to be questioned.

Keely forked one pork chop onto her plate, feeling guilty. Her dad kept glancing at her. He didn't say anything else, but Keely could read what was going through his mind.

"Look, girl, the best thing you have going for you is gymnastics," she could almost hear him say. "The truth is, you don't have your brother's brains. You have no other special talents. But you could make your mark in the world if you stayed slim and became a world-class gymnast. That's your one chance for the big brass ring . . ."

Keely couldn't enjoy the pork chop. She nibbled at it, feeling guilty again. She could almost feel the fat oozing into her body, plumping out her thighs with every morsel she put into her mouth. She ate a little salad, then pushed away from the table when her mom brought out the dessert—peach cobbler.

"I'm too full for dessert, Mom," Keely lied.

"You feeling okay?" her mom asked.

"Uh, yeah. I think I'll go study for my history test," Keely said. She wouldn't really study, though. She was too stressed and tired to study. She had to get away from the table because she couldn't bear looking at those luscious pork chops and being scared to eat another one. She couldn't stand staring at her mom's wonderful peach cobbler, watching her parents enjoy it, and being afraid to take one bite.

Piled on Keely's dresser in her bedroom were books and magazines about gymnastics. She loved reading about the stars of the sport.

It surprised Keely to read that the girls who won medals in gymnastics weren't always skinny little waifs, sprinting to glory on stick legs. At one time, full-bodied women excelled in the sport. Keely had read in astonishment that in

1968, an average, healthy woman named Vera Caslavska won the All-Around title at the Olympics in Mexico City. She was 5 foot 3, and she actually weighed 121 pounds! She was more than 20 pounds heavier than Keely and only two inches taller. Vera was only the second gymnast in history to win back-to-back Olympic All-Around titles, and she was average in size!

But then the skinny girls came. In the 1972 Olympics, Olga Korbut from the Soviet Union weighed only 85 pounds. Then came Cathy Rigby, the first U.S. woman to win a world medal, who looked like a little blonde doll. Mary Lou Retton looked more muscular, but she carried just 94 pounds on her 4 foot 10 inch frame.

Most of the girls looked like sprites.

Keely went into the bathroom and stepped on the scale again.

One hundred pounds!

Keely had gained a pound since coming home! That one miserable pork chop, she thought in horror. She'd been right about it. The calories had started pouring into her body the minute she sank her teeth into it.

Keely desperately closed the door. She turned on the water faucet in the basin and let it run hard. Then she knelt in front of the toilet. She stuck her finger down her throat. She gagged.

How does Liza do this? she thought.

Keely tried again, and this time she threw up. She hated it. She had never vomited on purpose before. She hadn't vomited at all since two years ago, and that was when she had food poisoning. It was such a horrible feeling.

Keely rinsed out her mouth with several glasses of water. Then she grabbed the room freshener and sprayed it all over the bathroom.

She leaned on the sink, feeling weak. But she felt something else too—light. She had gotten rid of the calorie-laden pork chop and the potatoes. Even the salad! It was all gone. The enemy had left her body. When she stepped onto the scales again, she weighed only 98 pounds.

Keely felt a sense of elation. She went to her bedroom and opened her history book. But she couldn't concentrate. She closed it again and got a book on Nadia Comaneci. Her eyes savored all the colored action pictures of the Romanian girl springing to the beam, flying in midair. In the 1976 Olympics, she received seven scores of perfect 10. How beautiful and triumphant she looked!

Keely hurried to the full-length mirror in her room.

"I only weigh 98 pounds," she groaned, "but I still look fat!"

* * *

When Keely saw Liza at school the next day, she pulled Liza aside and said, "I did it."

"What'd you do?" Liza asked.

"I made myself . . . you know . . . throw up," Keely said. "But it was really gross. I hated it."

"Oh, you get used to it," Liza said. "And it worked, right? It's the only way to do it. Laxatives give you cramps, and just not eating makes you look awful. You can eat all you want and then 'whoosh,' it's gone. Sometimes I really go all out. I'll eat two cheeseburgers and a chocolate shake. And then I get rid of it all. It's sort of like having your cake and eating it too!"

Keely looked at Liza. "How much do you weigh?" she asked.

"Eighty-five pounds," Liza said with pride.

"Eighty-five pounds! No way! You're almost as tall as me!" Keely cried covetously.

"Keely, I'm not even 5 feet tall," Liza said. But Keely didn't even seem to hear her.

"Wow . . . if I can just lose three more pounds. Then Wassily would be so proud of me. I'd finally look good in my leotard," Keely said.

"Oh, we're going to be late for history!" Liza suddenly groaned, looking at her watch. They knew Ms. Burks did not tolerate tardiness.

Both girls ran down the hall toward history class. The shrill bell caught them as they came bursting through the door. The girls scrambled for their seats.

"Not so fast, ladies," Ms. Burks said sharply. "Go to the office and get tardy slips."

The tests were already being passed out. Ms. Burks gave really long and difficult essay tests. Students needed every minute of the period to work on them. Going all the way to the office and back again with tardy slips would take at least ten minutes.

Keely and Liza rushed to the office and stood in line to get their tardy slips. Then they ran back to history class. By the time they got their tests, they had lost 15 minutes of precious time.

Keely was so stressed that the questions blurred before her eyes. She hadn't really studied the three chapters that were assigned. Now she had lost all hope of passing the test. It was futile. There simply wasn't time to make even good guesses. There were questions about Athens and Sparta and Persia. The test may as well have been written in Greek for all Keely knew.

After class, as Keely slumped out of the classroom, she saw Julio coming toward her.

"How was the test?" he asked.

"Horrible," moaned Keely. "I blew it completely. I didn't know anything."

"Too bad," Julio said. "But it's just one test. There'll be others. Hey, are you coming to the football game Friday night? My brother is starting as quarterback. It's the big grudge game with the Raiders."

"No, I've got to practice really late Friday at the gym. I'll be there until 9:00 at least," Keely replied. "We're practicing on the beam, and that's my weakest apparatus. Wassily is really on my case about it. It's so narrow, and it's so far off the ground. I'm kind of scared of it. I fell off it once and really got bruised up. So I really need to practice."

"Girl, that gymnastics is like a monster eating up all your time," said Julio. "I can't remember the last time you even came to a game or a party."

"Julio, you *know* how important gymnastics is to me. Unless I train really, really hard, I don't stand a chance of making it to the very top," Keely said.

"I don't know," Julio said. "It seems kind of stupid to let something like that take up your whole life when there's not much of a chance you'll even get to the top. My brother plays football. But he does other stuff, too, because he'll probably never be going to the NFL."

"That's a defeatist attitude," Keely said, parroting what her father had said so often. "You must never admit the possibility that you might not win. I'll be 16 when the Olympic games are held, and that's the best age for a girl in gymnastics. Mary Lou Retton won her gold medal when she was 16. Wassily said it's possible for me to be ready for the Olympics in two years."

"Wassily, Wassily," Julio complained bitterly. "I am so sick of hearing about that guy. The couple of times I watched you practice, I wanted to throttle the guy. He treats you like dirt. He yells and screams at you like some crazed lunatic. If the teachers at school treated students like that, they'd be fired."

"Wassily is doing that for our own good," Keely said. She always felt defensive when it came to her coach. "He knows how tough the competition is. If we're not perfect, then we don't stand a chance."

"Well, I hope you at least make it to my birthday party next month," Julio said.

"Oh, I wouldn't miss that," Keely promised.

Julio came a little closer to Keely then. "Have you lost some weight?" he asked her.

A thrill of joy went through Keely's heart. It showed! Even Julio was noticing the pounds dropping off. Surely Wassily would see it too. And he'd be delighted.

"Maybe I lost a little," Keely said.

"I don't like it that you're losing weight, Keely," Julio said. "You don't look so healthy. You hear what I'm saying? You're already too skinny. You're not doing anything stupid, like taking diet pills or something, are you?"

"Oh, no," Keely said.

"Well, you take care of yourself. You've got dark shadows under your eyes. That doesn't look good. I don't want you wasting away, you hear?" Julio said, real concern in his voice.

Keely smiled at the boy. He was sweet. But he didn't understand.

3

Keely's mother picked her up from school at 3:30.

"We'll stop for something to eat, honey, and then I'll take you over to the gym," Mrs. Wayne said. "I know you don't like school food, so you probably didn't eat much at lunch. What do you feel like? A burger, or chicken, or maybe Chinese? We could get some orange chicken at that little Chinese takeout."

"I'm not very hungry, Mom," Keely lied. For lunch at school she had eaten four carrot sticks.

"Well, you need to eat something," her mom said. "You'll be working hard at the gym, and you can't run without fuel."

"I had a huge lunch," Keely said, lying again.

Mrs. Wayne glanced over at her daughter. "Honey, you look tired," she said. "I hope gymnastics isn't taking too much out of you."

"No, Mom, I'm fine," Keely said. She decided to change the subject. "I'm really excited about going on tour."

"I know, Keely, but if you run down your health, you're not going anywhere,"

Mrs. Wayne said, pulling into the Chinese restaurant. She bought two buckets of orange chicken and handed one to Keely.

"Thanks, Mom. I'll eat this at the gym," Keely said.

"Be sure you do. I don't want you running yourself into some illness," her mom said.

Keely kept stealing glances at her mother. She was wearing a white tank top and blue shorts. She was 36 years old. Now that Keely thought about it, most people thought she was much younger than that. When she came to the last parents' night at school, a teacher actually thought she was one of the seniors.

When the family went to the beach last summer, a group of college guys were whistling at Keely's mom in her swimsuit. Her dad was really annoyed, but Keely could tell her mom was pleased. Mom *was* pretty, Keely thought.

But she was too fat . . .

Wasn't she?

Keely's mom pulled up in front of the gym. Keely grabbed her bag and jumped out.

"Keely, you forgot your orange chicken," her mom yelled after her.

"Oh, yeah," Keely said, coming back for the little bucket. It looked so good—the shiny pieces of chicken, the rich, tangy sauce. Keely was dying to eat some. She wanted to sit down in a dark corner and gobble down the whole bucket.

But, Keely thought, there must be thousands of calories in that bucket. She didn't dare eat any.

Addy ran up to Keely as she came in. "What's in the carton?" she asked.

"Mom got me some orange chicken, but I shouldn't eat any," Keely said. "I can just picture myself blowing up like a balloon."

"Oh, that stuff isn't fattening," Addy said. She looked around stealthily. "Wassily isn't here yet. Let's sit over there and split the chicken. It looks fantastic, and I am starving!"

"*You'd* eat it?" Keely asked in amazement.

"Sure," said Addy. "I've got to eat something. I've got a headache from not eating anything all day. If I don't get some food, I'll be so weak that I'll fall off the beam! Tonight I'll run six miles and get all the calories burned up anyway."

The girls sat down and began eating the orange chicken. It tasted even better than it looked. Keely could not remember eating such delicious food in a long time. She just kept grabbing pieces until she and Addy had emptied the carton.

"Well," Wassily said, springing up from nowhere, "I see my little portly piggies are stuffing themselves." He had been in the office and had snuck up behind the girls.

Keely was mortified. She didn't want to let Wassily down. If he lost faith in her, then she never would get to the Olympics. She would be a failure. Her father would be so disappointed in her. Wassily had often said he would not waste his time with girls who couldn't bring home the gold.

"Oh, Wassily, this is the first food I've had all day," she cried. "Honest. I just had orange juice for breakfast and a couple of carrot sticks for lunch . . ."

"Put on your leotards, girls," Wassily said. "If you can still fit in them, that is!" There was contempt in the man's voice.

Wassily was a tall, dark-haired handsome man, about 47 years old. He wanted to coach a gold medalist more than he wanted anything else in the world. As a youth, he had won a bronze medal in the Olympics track and field competition. He was bitter that he had not won the gold. Now he wanted the gold as a coach.

Keely went into the locker room and slipped into her leotard, shaking with apprehension. She didn't know if the orange chicken had already translated into fat. She didn't think it could be already on her hips. Still, when she looked down at her thighs, they seemed bloated and hideous.

How could that be? Keely thought in desperation.

When the girls emerged from the locker room, Wassily put his hands on his hips and stared at Keely. He shook his head. "Do you see the flab, little fatso? Were all those burgers and fries worth it?" he asked, belittling her.

"I . . . I . . . don't eat burgers and fries," Keely said, tears starting to fill her eyes and burn their way down her cheeks. "I haven't had a burger or fries in months. I swear it!"

"You need to run more," Wassily scolded. "How far do you run every day?"

"Uh . . . a couple of miles," Keely said.

Wassily turned to Addy. "How far do you run?" he asked.

"I run about six miles most days," Addy said.

"Good," Wassily said, turning again to Keely. "You see how attractive Adrienne's legs are? You must run more. Run, run!"

Keely was so upset by Wassily's harshness that it was hard to concentrate on her exercises. But she went through her floor routine without trouble.

The routine only lasted a little over a minute. But what was packed into those 80 seconds took thousands of hours to perfect.

The routine had to cover the entire floor, which was a 40-foot by 40-foot mat. It had to contain advanced acrobatics and gymnastics. It had to change directions and level of movement. And on top of it all, the gymnast had to be a dancer, showing a command of music, rhythm, and space.

When Keely began working on the balance beam, Wassily yelled at her for being sloppy. Keely tried to imagine the beam as being four feet wide instead of four inches. That's what a gymnast had to do—give the impression that she was performing on a much-wider surface. But it was hard. Especially when she forgot to not look down.

Keely did a two-foot takeoff into a punch somersault, known as a *punch front*.

"Better, but still too weak!" Wassily yelled.

Keely bit her lip and went grimly on.

"Do the Omelianchik!" instructed Wassily.

Keely took a deep breath. Then she did a back dive with a quarter twist, ending in a handstand. And she didn't fall! Keely let a small smile form on her lips, only to be scared away by Wassily's "Toes! Toes! Don't forget to point your toes! I swear, you are hopeless!"

Lastly, Keely performed the one stunt she felt confident with—the Korbut flic. She did a back dive to her hands. Then she swung down to finish, straddling the beam.

"Yes, that was good," said Wassily. "But your routine needs much more practice!"

Wassily then went to help Addy with the vault. Keely stayed and worked on the beam.

Then, about 15 minutes before the end of the practice session, Wassily called Addy, Keely, and Liza over. "You three are the best," he said. "Any one of you, with concentration and determination, should be able to win major competition. But you must work like crazy now. In the summer, if you are very good, you will go on tour. Then the Olympic Trials. It is all possible. It is in your hands."

Keely's heart was racing. She had been in minor competitions before, and she had won a few times. But the competition was fairly light. Soon she would be facing girls with as much skill as herself, or more.

* * *

As the Wayne family sat down to dinner that night, Keely told her parents what Wassily had said.

"I could really end up going to the Olympics," Keely said.

"That's wonderful, Keely," her dad said as he spread butter on his biscuit. Keely's gaze followed the butter off the edge of the knife to the white, hot heart of one of her mom's wonderful biscuits. She could taste it! Keely longed for a piece of the flaky biscuit, but she didn't dare try it.

"Honey, you aren't touching your lamb chops," her mom said. "They have plenty of applesauce on them, just the way you like them."

"Just quit nagging her, Jill," Keely's dad admonished. "Keely knows what she's doing. Right, Keely?"

"Yeah, Dad," Keely said. But she didn't look at him.

"I thought so," he said. "You know what it takes to get to the top." Then he glanced at his watch. "Listen, girls, sorry, but I can't finish supper with you," he said, wiping his mouth. "I've got a meeting, and if I don't leave now, I'll be late."

Mr. Wayne kissed Keely and his wife good-bye and scurried out the door.

Keely picked up one lamb chop and nibbled on it. She found it so delicious that she quickly finished it and reached for another. She ate some yams, too, and a quarter of an apple turnover.

It's all right, Keely told herself. She didn't have to starve herself. Didn't Liza say she ate anything she wanted and then just "took care of it"? Keely dreaded the trip to the bathroom, but she was enjoying the good food so much.

When Keely finally pushed away from the table, she said, "I think I'll go for a little jog."

"It's dark outside, Keely," Mrs. Wayne said. "I don't like you running in the dark."

"I'll stay right on our street, Mom," Keely said. If she exercised her dinner off, then maybe she wouldn't have to stick her finger down her throat tonight.

Keely headed out into the cool darkness. Looking around, she thought she saw someone standing outside at the house next door. After her eyes adjusted to the dark, Keely saw that it was Sandra Ashton.

Sandra was a ballet teacher, and Keely used to be in her class when she was seven. Sandra had started working in her mother's dance studio when she was a freshman, and she was only in her early twenties now. Sandra also sang in the same church choir as Keely.

Keely had always thought Sandra Ashton was the most beautiful girl she had ever seen. She had smooth, satiny brown skin and high, regal cheekbones.

"Hi, Sandra!" Keely called out. "I haven't seen you in church lately. We miss you in the choir. You were the best soprano."

"Yeah, I've been going to Los Angeles to audition for a part in a musical," said Sandra, jogging over to meet Keely. "Maybe it's my big break. I haven't had time for anything else."

Sandra had always had a spectacular figure. Even now in the darkness, Keely could see her slender lines. "Wow, Sandra," Keely said, "how do you stay so skinny?"

Sandra laughed. "I'm a dancer, Keely," she said. "I have to stay in shape. I bet you've never seen a fat dancer, and you never will. I eat a lot of salads, fish, and chicken. And I run a lot of miles."

"I've got to keep my weight down, too, in gymnastics," Keely said.

"You look terrific, Keely," Sandra said. But Keely thought she was only saying that to be nice. Sandra was always so kind. That's why the kids in ballet class loved her so much. No matter how clumsy they were, she was always patient with them.

"I need to lose a few more pounds," Keely said. "The trouble is that I really like to eat. And Mom is such a good cook. It's hard to sit there and see all that delicious stuff and not eat much of it."

Sandra came a little closer. "Honey, what you've got to do is psyche yourself out," she said. "Convince yourself how disgusting it is to eat too much. That's what I did. Every bite I took, I pictured fat globules sticking to my body. It got so that I had to force myself to eat *anything*. I'm not even tempted to overeat anymore. Food used to be a big pleasure in my life, but now I don't even think about it. I eat enough to live, but I don't live to eat anymore."

"You're lucky to be like that," Keely said.

"It has nothing to do with luck," answered Sandra. "You've got to work at it. Just keep your goals in mind. I want to be a famous dancer, and so I think about that all the time. I think about how important it is to be slim and attractive. When I see food, it's a barrier to my dreams. I won't let it block me. You have to imagine yourself standing on that platform at the Olympics getting the gold medal with the national anthem playing . . . then you'll never want to stuff yourself again."

Sandra said good-bye and jogged on then. She was so tall and willowy. Keely envied her. It must be wonderful, Keely thought, to be so tall with lovely long legs . . .

But Sandra couldn't be a gymnast, Keely thought.

That was for small-framed girls like Keely.

Keely was exhausted when she got home. She showered and went to bed. But she didn't get much rest. She had a horrible nightmare. She was in some sort of a restaurant, and the waitresses kept bringing piles of food on huge trays. Keely could not stop eating. She had never seen such food. Marvelous giant shrimp scampi in butter sauce, sirloin steaks dripping with gravy, and pork chops and candied yams.

Suddenly, there was Wassily, his face on fire with rage. He seemed like an avenging spirit.

"How could you do this?" Wassily screamed at Keely. "Now it is over for you. You have no chance to be a great gymnast. Look at you! You are a fat pig!"

"I'll lose all the weight I gained," Keeley cried. "I swear I will! I know how to do it now."

"You pig!" Wassily thundered at her. "You have ruined the chances we both had for glory. I would have shared in the great moment. I am your coach. The whole world would be looking at me too. You have destroyed your dream, and you have stolen mine too!"

"Nooo, I can fix it! I swear I can be thin again," Keely sobbed.

Keely awoke with a start and sat up in bed, shaking. Her face was wet with tears.

She scrambled from bed and ran to the bathroom to weigh herself. It was only a dream, but she had to prove to herself that she hadn't gained any weight.

Keely stared down at the big, black numbers.

One hundred one pounds!

"No, no, no," Keely groaned, clenching her fists.

4

At breakfast Keely's mom took a long look at Keely. "I don't think you slept well last night," she said. "You have dark circles under your eyes."

"I guess I had nightmares or something," Keely said. She picked out segments of her grapefruit.

"I hope you're not pushing too hard with your training, and your schoolwork on top of that," Mrs. Wayne said. "I hope you're not getting your hopes up too high, either. There must be millions of girls in gymnastics, and only a few of them become famous."

"Now, Jill," Mr. Wayne said, walking into the kitchen, "don't be negative. Negativity is a killer. Nobody is going to accomplish anything in this world with a negative attitude. There's no reason why our little girl can't go right to the top just like Mary Lou Retton and that little gal who won a gold medal with an injured ankle." He looked reproachfully at his wife.

"Well, I don't want her sacrificing her whole childhood," Keely's mom argued.

Keely's dad turned to Keely, a big smile on his face. "There's no place you'd rather be than in that gym training your little heart out for a go at the gold. Am I right, Keely?" he asked.

Keely smiled back because she knew that was what her dad expected. "Yeah," she said. Her father would never raise a hand to her. But when he got that stern, disappointed look on his face, Keely crumbled inside like an autumn leaf under a heavy boot.

"Then it's unanimous," her dad said.

Keely had once loved gymnastics more than anything. But that was before she had gotten really good. She had been just playing for fun then, and maybe a few small prizes. Keely had loved to watch the competitions on television and then go try the routines herself. She dreamed of being like those magical girls who flew through the air, defying gravity in their gorgeous leotards.

It had been such fun in the beginning.

Now it was scary.

But even now in her heart, Keely knew that winning the gold medal at the Olympics had to be the most exciting thing that could happen to a young girl.

She knew that if it happened to her, she'd probably remember it as the most incredible moment of her life. Even when she got to be an old lady.

But the fear was growing—especially the fear of turning into a roly-poly girl to the disgust and disappointment of Wassily and her dad. How could they ever forgive her if she undermined herself like that? How could Keely ever forgive herself if she let her love for food stand in her way of such a grandiose dream?

Sandra was right, Keely thought. She had to learn to hate food too. She needed to hate it as much as she now loved it. She had to see food as horrible and revolting. When she looked at a cheesecake or a pork chop, she had to see big globs of fat waiting to attach themselves like parasites to her body.

Now Keely looked down at her sunny-side up eggs. She pictured them stuck to her thighs, dripping yellow yolk down her legs.

"I'm not very hungry this morning," Keely said. She had stuck her fork in the eggs and scattered them around so it looked like she'd eaten some.

"You're feeling OK, aren't you?" her mom asked.

"Yeah, I'm feeling fine," Keely said. Actually she had a headache and was a little dizzy. She went in the bathroom and took some vitamins with a big glass of water. Then she slung on her backpack and headed for school.

Ms. Burks returned the history tests that morning. Keely had scored 60 out of a possible 100—an *F*. That was the worst grade she had ever gotten in her life. Her heart sank. She knew that when you got an *F*, the teacher usually got in touch with your parents.

The bell rang. Merriann, who sat next to Keely, gasped. She had seen Keely's *F* written in red ink on the top of her paper. "Wow, you flunked," she said. "You never flunk a test!"

"I'm concentrating on gymnastics," Keely explained, trying to justify her failure. "I'm spending four hours a day training, and now I need to practice even more. School is just in the way. I'll probably have to drop school and take home-study courses pretty soon."

"You'd drop high school?" Merriann asked, wide-eyed. "You mean you wouldn't come to West Bluff *at all* anymore?"

"I need to train harder," said Keely. "I'm hopefully going on tour this summer. I need to get ready for the Olympic Trials."

Merriann and Keely had been friends since third grade.

"I'll miss you if you don't come anymore," Merriann said.

"I'll miss you, too, Merri," Keely said. "But it's something I have to do. I'm 14, and if I don't throw myself into this full time, then I won't have a chance to make the Olympics in two years. The girls getting the gold medals are younger and younger. It used to be women in their twenties. In 1968 it was this lady who was 26 years old—almost twice my age!"

"I'd be scared stiff to fly through the air like you do. To jump on those bars and stuff," Merriann said.

"It's my gift," Keely said. "Dad says that everybody has some sort of gift, and that's mine. I really don't have anything else that's special. My brother is smarter and better looking than me. And he's never shy like I am."

"Well, high school won't be near as much fun for me if you're not here," Merriann said.

* * *

When Keely got home from gymnastics practice that night, her mom was waiting for her with a serious look on her face. "I got a phone call from your history teacher this afternoon," she said. "Ms. Burks says you're failing history. I was really shocked."

"I'm sorry, Mom, but I just got so mixed up on that last test that it brought my grade way down," Keely said.

"Ms. Burks said you didn't turn in your last project, either . . . something about current events," her mom said.

"Oh, yeah, well, I was so busy—" Keely said.

"That's no excuse. I don't want your gymnastics to cause you to fail high school," Keely's mom interrupted. "Education is just too important."

"It's okay, Mom," said Keely. "Wassily said he's going to talk to you and Dad pretty soon about getting me into a home-study program so I don't have to go to classes anymore."

"Keely!" Mom cried. "You'd be missing all the fun and friendships of those high school years. Those were some of the best years of my life. I still have most of the friends I made in high school, and we still talk about the funny things that happened. I'd hate for you to miss all that."

"I have good friends on my team, Mom." Keely tried to convince her mom and herself. "Liza and Addy are really great friends, and we have so much in common. We'll all be dropping regular school and taking home study. We'll be on tour together."

"Are you sure that this is what you really want, Keely?" Her mom sighed.

"Sure, Mom," Keely replied. Although she wasn't really sure. "Liza and Addy are really close to me. They're coming over tomorrow morning, and we're all going shopping before practice. Addy just turned 16, and she's got her driver's license, so she can drive us to the mall. I'm really excited about that. I haven't been shopping for *ages*."

"I still don't know about the home study," said Mrs. Wayne. "We'll have to talk about it some more."

Keely had some grapefruit and low-fat cottage cheese for breakfast the next morning. Then Addy pulled up in her sleek little black car. Addy had long blonde hair that she always kept tightly tied back during exercise and competition. It made her look younger, more little-girlish.

Keely never told Addy, but she thought 16 was already a little old for getting a gold medal in two years. She'd be 18 then. Maybe, Keely thought, she had already missed the boat. Liza and Keely had much better odds because they were both 14. But Addy *looked* so pretty and dainty that sometimes she passed for 12. So it was possible she could still make it, even though she was sort of old.

Liza was dark, with short, curly brown hair. Keely thought both Addy and Liza had better figures than she did. But Keely was the best athlete. Deep in Keely's heart, she thought that she had the best chance among the three of getting to the Olympics.

"Let's go!" Addy shouted as the trio set out for the mall on Saturday. "I'm in the mood to shop. There's a sale, and I'm dying for a new pair of jeans. We've got to get there before all the small sizes are gone."

"Yeah," Liza laughed, "it seems like they make tons of jeans for really big girls, and we end up fighting over a few pairs."

"That's because most girls are overweight," Keely said, feeling a sense of superiority over the fuller-figured girls. "Dad said that he saw on TV that obesity is the number one health problem in the country."

"Don't look at me," Liza said. "I'm one of those skinny girls who throws up a lot."

"Ewwww," Addy groaned, "that is just so gross. The way it smells, and it can't be healthy."

"Look who's talking," Liza said. "Little Miss Laxatives-by-the-Pound!"

"I'm trying to cut down on that," Addy said. "I run up and down the bleachers early in the morning before anybody else gets to school. I'm hoping that keeps my weight down."

"How about you, Keely?" Liza asked. "You look good."

"I try not to eat too much," Keely said nervously. "I saw a girl, an older girl, the other night. She has to be thin too, because she's a dancer. She told me you've got to convince yourself that food is just absolutely disgusting. Now she says she almost has to force herself to eat anything at all. And that really helps her stay skinny."

"Ohhhh, but chocolate chip cookies aren't disgusting," Liza groaned. "They're gooey and irresistible!"

"And fried chicken and mashed potatoes," Addy said.

"You've got to picture all that food stuck to your thighs. That's what Sandra told me," Keely said. "She said she's psyched herself out of eating much."

"You know what I hate?" Addy asked. "Weighing myself *all* the time. I swear I do it ten times a day. It's compulsive or something. I'm always worried that I've suddenly put on weight. So I've got to relieve my anxiety by running to the scales."

"Me too," Keely said. "It's the first thing I do in the morning and the last thing at night. Sometimes I'll get up in the middle of the night and weigh myself."

"Maybe we're all crazy," Addy said. "Maybe starving yourself makes you crazy."

The three girls laughed as Addy turned into the parking ramp at the mall.

When the girls entered the store, they immediately sought out the junior jeans department. Keely searched the jean racks and found the style she had been looking for. Most of the jeans there were sizes 11 and higher. "Oh, here's my 2," she cried, grabbing the jeans.

The three girls went into the dressing room to try on their jeans. When Keely slipped into hers, they felt tight! A jolt of panic went through her.

"You guys! Why are these jeans so tight?" she cried. "I always wear size 2 or smaller!"

"Sometimes they make a mistake on the tag," Addy said. "Go get another 2. Or maybe they're making the sizes smaller."

Addy stood before the mirror in her jeans. She looked spectacular. She spun around, smiling. "These are almost too big for me!"

"Addy, you look great," Liza said, slipping into lighter-colored jeans.

Keely dressed and raced back to the racks, looking for another size 2. When she returned to the dressing room, Liza was looking in the mirror.

"Are you sure these jeans look good on me?" Liza asked. The small size couldn't have fit better.

Keely broke out in a cold sweat as she pulled on the new jeans she had just gotten off the racks. She sucked in her breath, trying to make herself thinner.

But the jeans felt too tight!

It couldn't be, Keely told herself in anguish. She wasn't eating anything! She was hungry all the time.

She couldn't have gained a jeans size in just a month. Not on grapefruit slices . . .

5 "There's something wrong with these jeans!" Keely cried, rushing to put her own pants back on. She had weighed herself just last night, and she was down to 99 pounds. "I'm putting these back. The tags must be all screwed up."

When Keely returned to the dressing room again, this time with a shirt, she overheard her friends talking about her. Keely froze outside the door. She didn't want to hear anything bad, but she was unable to resist listening.

"Keely's problem is that she's kind of muscular," Liza was saying. "She's always going to look fatter than us no matter what she weighs because of that."

"I'm glad I don't have that problem," Addy said.

"Yeah, me too," Liza said. "Poor girl. It must be awful to starve yourself and stuff and still look pudgy."

When Keely finally opened the door to the dressing room, she pretended she hadn't heard anything. It would have just made things awkward if Liza and Addy knew she'd heard them. Anyway, they weren't trying to be mean and catty. They were just being honest.

But Keely was hurt deeply. No matter what she did, she was cursed with genetically fat, bulky thighs.

She'd lose more than five pounds, she vowed. That would be an improvement. It just had to be!

When Keely tried on a pair of jeans in size 4, they fit well. Keely didn't tell the other girls she had taken a size up. "You were right. The tags were wrong," she lied. "These are my regular size, and they fit perfectly."

"Those jeans really look good on you, Keely," Liza said. "With jeans like that and this shirt you picked out, you'll be incredible!"

"Yeah, terrific," Addy added.

The girls shopped for another hour. Then they stopped at a frozen yogurt store.

"I am starving," Liza said. "I need something before practice. I'm just getting a small plain vanilla."

"I'm getting some nuts with mine," Addy said. "I don't care. I have to have some nuts! I'll just run 50 miles tonight to get rid of the calories."

"Fifty miles?" Liza laughed.

"Well, it feels like that sometimes. I think I'm just going to drop from exhaustion one of these days. And then I'll be dead. And they can put on my tombstone that I was going for the gold and got marble instead—a marble grave marker," Addy said, giggling.

"Oh, Addy, you're terrible," Liza laughed.

"I'm not having anything," Keely said. "I had a huge breakfast this morning. Hotcakes and sausages, and oatmeal, and . . ." Keely lied.

"I don't believe it," Liza howled. "You eat sausages?"

"Well, I have to eat them when Mom makes such a good breakfast," Keely said. "I can't hurt her feelings. It's really hard. I think I'll just have a glass of ice water."

The three girls sat at one of the outdoor tables. Addy and Liza ate their yogurts, and Keely sipped on ice water. But she longed with all her heart for a taste of that yogurt. She watched every delicious bite disappear into her friends' mouths. She ached with hunger and her mouth watered, but she didn't dare eat anything when her jeans size went up like that.

Keely so envied her friends with their naturally slimmer figures. Once she had complained to Wassily about being so muscular.

"Look at the pictures of Mary Lou Retton," he had said. "She won the gold medal before you were born, but look at her. She had muscles. But she watched her diet. That's what you must do."

* * *

The practice sessions at the gym became more intense as the time for the invitational drew near. High school students and young women from all over the country would be competing.

Wassily expected spartan attitudes from the girls. Keely focused on what she knew was so important. She worked to please her coach, her dad, and lastly herself. And throughout it all, she ignored the pangs of hunger that attacked her famished body.

When that Saturday morning finally arrived, Keely was extremely nervous. She felt she had mastered all four apparatuses. The vaults, the bars, the balance beam, and the floor. But would she be good enough?

They all rode to the competition in a van owned by Wassily's gym. No one talked much. Keely tried to squelch her gurgling stomach. She had eaten even less than normal the past few days. She wanted to make sure she looked good for the judges.

Keely, Liza, and Addy all wished one another luck, but they didn't mean it. Each just wanted to win, that's all. Never mind who lost.

Keely knew that Addy, with her long limbs, would look better on the uneven bars. And Liza was a better dancer for the floor exercises. But Keely had a lot of power. She hoped to run up the points with a strong performance on the vault.

Routines on the uneven bars, balance beam, and floor exercises all started with a point value of 9.00. A gymnast could earn an additional 1.00 point by performing special combinations or more difficult elements. Each apparatus had required elements that must be performed or a reduction in points would occur. Any faults in the routine would also result in point reductions.

Keely would perform two different vault routines. The scores from each vault would be accepted and averaged. Gymnasts could choose which stunts they wished to perform.

This meet followed the Olympic order of events. That meant that each gymnast would perform in the order of vault, uneven bars, balance beam, and then floor exercises.

Watching the other gymnasts warm up, Keely was surprised at the level of skill. She knew that other Olympic hopefuls would be attending the invitational, but she hadn't really been nervous about the competition until now.

When it came to Keely's turn on the vault, she walked to the top of the runway and took her position. The green flag was waved and Keely stared at the vaulting horse ahead. She began her approach.

She sprinted forward on the 80-foot-long carpet. She performed a strong handspring onto the springboard to propel herself onto and over the vault. She completed her preflight by touching the vault with both hands. Then she pushed off the vault into a piked front somersault. But halfway through the half-twist at the end, her legs spread. She felt it happening, and she wanted to scream in frustration. Keely landed, her feet pointing in different directions.

Keely knew that her errors meant deductions. Her leg separation would be at least a 0.15 point deduction. Her poor foot form on her dismount would cost her at least 0.20 points.

She glanced at Wassily. Disgust crawled all over his face.

"Oh no, oh no," a little voice inside Keely's head chanted, "now you've done it. You've embarrassed Wassily. You've embarrassed yourself."

She tried to push her mistakes out of her mind. She had to concentrate for her second attempt at the vault. But the look on Wassily's face seemed branded in her memory.

Keely's second attempt was better. But this time she didn't get the high amplitude she needed in the afterflight phase of her vault. However, she managed to stick her landing.

Keely tried not to look at her parents, who were watching in the stands. She sat down heavily on the sidelines and watched the other girls. Tears ran down her face. Addy and Liza tried to comfort her.

"It's only the first apparatus," said Addy.

"Yeah," said Liza. "You'll nail your other routines."

Despite Keely's shaky start, she performed fairly well on the other apparatuses. Her routine on the uneven bars flowed from one movement to the next. She was even able to stay in the handstand position in one of her swings longer than ever before in practice. Even on the balance beam, Keely surprised herself. She received only a few minor deductions for bent knees and a slight hop on her dismount. By the time she was to perform her floor routine, she had gained considerable confidence. She had even extracted a few “oohs” and “ahhs” from the crowd.

When the standings were officially posted, Addy had finished fourteenth, Liza seventh, and Keely had made it in the top ten, finishing tenth. Her high scores in the uneven bars and floor exercises had made up for her sloppy vaults.

“Keely, you made the cut!” Liza cried. The top ten finishers at the invitational would get automatic invitations to the tour this summer.

Keely leaped to her feet and screamed.

“Calm down,” Wassily said scornfully, “it is nothing to brag about. You were terrible. You all shamed me. The competition stunk, and yet you, Keely and Liza, barely made it by the skin of your teeth. Addy, you must now work ten times harder to even stay in my class. You all must devote eight hours a day to practicing. Forget school. Forget everything but the gym.”

The girls rode in the van back to West Bluff to meet their parents. Keely’s parents followed the van back to the school.

Addy was remarkably calm for her poor showing as they rode in the van. "I guess in a way it's a relief. Maybe I'm just no good and I can relax a little," she said.

"Addy!" Liza cried. "Don't give up. You could still go on the tour with us if you just practiced really hard."

Addy put her face in her hands and wept. "I'm tired of it. I'm tired of running until I'm ready to drop. I'm tired of all those laxatives and having to be scared every time I eat. I'm tired of my parents expecting me to be a big international star and get my face on cereal boxes. I'm just not good enough. Don't you guys see? I'm not good enough."

Liza and Keely put their arms around Addy.

"You *are* good enough," Liza said. "Hang in there. You can do it. We're all going through the same thing."

"And you're so poised," Keely said. "You looked so graceful in the floor exercises."

"I'm sick of missing out on all the parties and the beach picnics and time with my friends," Addy groaned.

"You're just feeling down right now. You'll feel different tomorrow," Liza promised.

The van pulled into the parking lot at West Bluff High School. Addy was the first out. She spotted her mother waiting, leaning on her car.

"Mom, I'm *sorry*," Addy cried. "I'm sorry."

Addy had told Keely that Mrs. Thorn had taken time off from her busy career as a real estate broker to watch the invitational. A lot of parents had come, Keely noticed. But she knew Mrs. Thorn was neglecting important clients to watch her daughter finish fourteenth in the standings.

"I'm sorry too," Mrs. Thorn said. "You just weren't focused. What on earth got into you?"

"I trained so hard, and then when I had to actually perform, I froze," Addy said, crying softly.

"Come on," Mrs. Thorn said, "just get in the car." She sounded angry and disappointed. Keely remembered Addy telling her once that her new car had been a gift on the condition that Addy train really hard in gymnastics. It was sort of like a carrot they held in front of her face.

As Addy and her mother left, Liza said, "My parents aren't like that. They don't push me so hard. I feel sorry for Addy. I just love gymnastics so much that I got in deeper and deeper . . ."

"Yeah, that's how it is with me too," Keely said. "My parents are behind me, but they're not putting on any pressure."

Keely was lying, of course. Her mom didn't put any pressure on. But her dad had his heart set on going to the Olympics two years from now and watching the world cheer on his little girl.

"So," Mr. Wayne said on the ride home, "you finished tenth. Well, that's not exceptional, but it's better than finishing lower."

"Yeah, I didn't think I'd do that well," said Keely. "When my legs splayed out in my landing on the first vault, I was really scared that it was a telltale sign of the day. I thought it would drop me so far down that I couldn't make it up."

"Why did that happen, Keely?" her dad asked.

"I don't know. I guess it happens to the best sometimes," Keely said.

"It shouldn't, though," Mr. Wayne scolded. "There's no excuse for sloppy work." He didn't show anger. He never did. His voice was simply stern and critical. He made her feel like she had failed him *again*. And that hurt more than if he had yelled at her.

"I'll practice harder so it won't happen again," Keely promised quietly.

"Wassily will be coming over on Sunday," her dad said.

"When was that arranged?" her mom asked, a little annoyed. "I didn't know anything about it."

"He approached me after the meet. While you were helping Keely pack up her stuff," Keely's dad said. "I invited him over for Sunday dinner so we could talk about what's best for Keely. Wassily seems to think it's 'make or break' time. Either she's wholeheartedly into her sport, or she's never going to be good enough for a berth in the Olympics. Wassily thinks

Keely has a lot of talent. And she's got a real shot at the top, if only she can train more and conquer her tendency to overeat."

"But what does it mean—get 'wholeheartedly into her sport'?" Mrs. Wayne asked. "What does it mean for Keely?"

Keely had the strange feeling that, although they were discussing her life, Keely was not part of the decisions being made. Her dad was talking about her as if she weren't there. He was ticking off her failings like you would recite the shortcomings of a promising horse that has a shot at the Triple Crown.

"Wassily has a lot of issues he wants to run by us, Jill. He thinks now is the time Keely should quit regular classes at the high school and go with home study. He wants to know if we're on board for the tour this summer," Keely's dad said, turning finally to Keely. "And he wants us to make sure this little butterball keeps in shape before she gets too fat to compete."

"Now Peter," Keely's mom said. "Keely doesn't need to hear statements like that."

But she stopped her argument there because Keely's dad had given her *the look.*

Keely felt her resentment turn almost to hatred. Why did her dad insist on needling her about her weight? Didn't he realize she was nearly starving herself?

Her mom looked at Keely. "Honey, what do you think of all this?" she asked.

"Well, I—" Keely started to talk, but her father interrupted her.

"You want nothing more than to get your shot at Olympic gold. Am I right?" he asked. "You don't care what it takes—stopping regular school, dieting, exercising, the whole thing—if it means reaching your dream. Am I right?"

"Well, yeah," Keely acquisced.

"But you have to do your part, Keely. This is not going to be a walk in the park," her dad lectured. "Wassily told me that he came into the gym the other day and you and another girl were stuffing yourselves on some junk food. That has got to stop, okay? And Wassily said you're a whiner. When you fall and hurt yourself, you don't just go for the liniment and get back on the apparatus. You whine. That's not the stuff of champions, Keely. You have to be willing to sacrifice for this gold. You've got to be able to sacrifice until it hurts . . ."

Keely looked at her father in silence.

She didn't like him anymore.

6

Julio Healey sang in the church choir with Keely. He had a smooth tenor voice. The only times Keely saw Julio anymore were at church and school. Pretty soon she wouldn't even see him at school. It would just be at church. They used to hang out and go to parties and games and have a lot of fun with their choir group. But Keely hardly even had time anymore for the choir. She half-expected Wassily to insist that she drop that too.

"My birthday party was fun," Julio said before church on Sunday. His face showed disappointment. "I missed you, though."

"Oh, Julio! When was it?" Keely cried in a stricken voice. "I was going to come, but I forgot!"

"Friday night. It's okay. I know you're busy," Julio said. "So how's everything going?"

"Okay, I guess," Keely said. It hurt her to look at Julio and remember all the good times she'd had with him. Half a dozen friends would go to the beach or to a party and just kick back and listen to good music. Keely missed Julio. She missed Merriann and the whole gang.

Keely was sorry she'd ever taken up gymnastics. For a few bitter moments, she wished she'd never have to see Wassily or a vault or beam again.

But then she remembered how she dreamed of becoming so good that she would win a gold medal. She remembered her fantasies of being in the newspaper and on TV. And all the little girls running up to her for her autograph. She pictured her cheering section at the Olympics. All her family and friends waving little American flags. It would be so exciting, such a once-in-a-lifetime thing. And Keely did want that. *She still did want it . . .*

After church services, Keely had about an hour before she had to be home. She dreaded Sunday dinner with Wassily coming over.

"Let's go for a drive," Julio said.

"We can't go far. I've got to be home by 1:00. My coach is coming over," Keely said.

"We'll just drive down to the lake," Julio said.

They parked on a dirt turnoff overlooking the lake. The sky was very blue, and its bright color was reflected in the lake. The sunshine scattered diamonds in one corner of the little lake. "It's pretty, huh?" Keely said.

"Yeah," Julio said, his face pensive.

"A lot of the singers were missing from choir today," Keely said, just to fill the awkward silence with words. "Jeff didn't come, and Sandra wasn't there either. She has such a pure soprano. When we sang 'Amazing Grace,' I really missed the sound of her voice."

"Sandra's in the hospital," Julio said. "Reverend Paxton told me. I thought you knew it."

"In the hospital?" Keely exclaimed. "I don't believe it! I talked to her just the other night. We were both jogging. She looked terrific. She's so pretty. She was telling me about going to Los Angeles to audition for a musical. Are you sure you heard it right, Julio?"

"Yeah, I'm sure," said Julio. "Her parents had to take her to the hospital. She fainted, and they couldn't revive her right away. So I guess they're checking her out."

"I hope it's nothing serious," Keely said.

"Reverend Paxton said she was shopping with her mom and just fainted. Maybe it was too hot in the store or something. I don't know. But they're running tests," Julio said.

"She's so beautiful," Keely said, remembering how slim and lovely Sandra looked the other night. Those long, slender arms, the trim thighs in her pretty little shorts, the graceful swan neck.

"She's kind of bony," Julio said. "I noticed it the last time she sang in the choir. I thought she looked kind of *old*."

"Julio, she's only 22 or so," Keely said.

"Yeah, that's why I thought it was so weird that she looked so haggard and, you know . . . old," Julio said.

"Poor Sandra," Keely said. "I hope this doesn't ruin her chances to make that audition. She's such a sweet person."

"Keely, when that guy Wassily comes to your house today, is he going to talk your parents into pulling you out of school? Do you think that's what he's up to?" Julio suddenly asked.

Keely shrugged. "I'm not sure," she said. "I just need a lot more practice time if I'm going anywhere. Dad says gymnastics is my gift, my *only* gift."

"That's not true," Julio said, softly. "You've got plenty of gifts. You're nice and pretty. And you've got a good singing voice in the choir. Reverend Paxton says you sing with real feeling. That you've really got the spirit."

"You're sweet, Julio," Keely said, glancing at her watch. "We'd better be getting back. I don't want to get home late and have Wassily there already."

"You want to stop for a quick sundae or something?" Julio asked.

"Oh, no," Keely said. "I'll be eating a big dinner when I get home."

Julio turned and stared at Keely for a minute. "You know what, Keely? You don't look so good," he said. "You sure you've been eating well lately? I know how you worry about your weight. You haven't been dieting or something . . . have you?"

Keely laughed. "Oh, Julio. Mom just loads my plate with food, and I eat it clean. Honest I do," Keely said in a nervous voice.

"You always had a nice, healthy round face, and now I can see your cheekbones," Julio said.

"You're supposed to be able to see a girl's cheekbones, Julio. I'm losing my baby fat, that's all," Keely said.

"Well, I remember watching the Olympic Games last time, and all the girls looked really scrawny. I don't want you to look like that. They were around 16, but they looked about 10 years old. They didn't even have shapes like a girl should . . ." Julio said, flushing a little with embarrassment. "You know what I mean. I just hope you'd never do anything stupid just to stay skinny."

"Not me," Keely said in a shrill voice. Her voice always turned shrill when she was lying. "I love to eat too much. Ask anybody."

Keely ran down the walk to her house after Julio dropped her off. She found her mother preparing for Wassily's arrival. She was putting fresh flowers in the little floral vase in the middle of the table, and the best silverware was out. Keely could tell how much her parents respected Wassily. They didn't even put out the best silverware when Reverend Paxton came.

"Well, here you are, finally," Keely's dad said in an annoyed voice. "I thought maybe you'd forgotten who was coming over today."

"No," Keely said. She dreaded it so much, how could she forget it? She could imagine how it would be, sitting at the table while Wassily openly discussed all her faults. "You know, maybe I shouldn't even be here when he comes," she said.

"Nonsense," Mr. Wayne said. "We'll be making plans affecting your life, Keely."

Wassily arrived early with his pretty, slender wife, who wore her faded blonde hair atop her head.

"Emilia won the silver medal in gymnastics before we were married," Wassily said proudly. "It should have been the gold, but the judges were very bad that year."

"Yes, they were very unfair," Emilia agreed in a sharp, petulant voice, as if the slight had happened a week ago instead of decades ago.

Emilia Karpov had a still-attractive but wizened little face. It was like the face of a child that remained small even as it grew older. When she was competing in the Olympics, she must have been one of those big-eyed little waifs from Eastern Europe who rarely smiled, Keely guessed.

The pot roast, potatoes, and vegetables were put on the table and consumed—though not by Keely, except sparingly. Wassily then leaned back in his chair and got to the business at hand.

"You have heard of Diana Durham," Wassily said. "A very fine black gymnast of the past. African American, like Keely. She was great. But she missed Olympic gold. A little mistake here, an injury there. Keely has as much talent as Durham had."

"That is wonderful to hear," Keely's dad said, bursting with pride.

"But she also has problems, deep problems. And I do not know if they can be overcome," Wassily said, bringing a distraught look to Mr. Wayne's face. "I've already talked to you about how she is unwilling to work in pain. Real champions must work in pain. This little girl here, Keely, she can be a crybaby."

"Well, Keely, can we do something about that?" her dad asked.

Keely felt humiliated with both Wassily and her father staring at her as if she were algae under a microscope. She *often* worked in pain. She would just rub on liniment and go on. But a few times when she took a really nasty fall, maybe she did cry a little.

"It's up to you," her dad said. "Do you want to throw in the towel right now, or are you willing to toughen up, Keely?"

"I want to . . . you know . . . do what I have to," Keely said, trying to feign enthusiasm.

"And then she must watch her weight," Wassily said. "No pies, cookies, big cheeseburgers. Just fruit and lean meats and fish. There is no such thing as a chubby gymnast, and Keely tends to eat too much."

"I've noticed that she's eating much less lately," Keely's mom piped up. "I've even been worried about it."

"That is good," Wassily said. "Very good that she is eating more moderately."

"Yes, I've been telling her—only enough food for sustenance," Keely's dad eagerly interjected.

Keely felt a wave of bitterness. She had eaten hardly anything in such a long time. Why didn't her dad notice?

"Then there is school," Wassily said. "A gymnast who is training to full capacity cannot go to regular classes."

"Yes," Keely's mom said. "That has been a problem. Keely is failing history."

"Well, I will help you make all the arrangements," Wassily said. "She can take a home-study course and not have to report to classes anymore. She can fit her schoolwork into times when she is not training."

"That sounds good to me," Keely's dad said. "When does all this start?" He did not ask Keely how she felt. No one did.

"One more week of regular school is all she must take," Wassily said. "Then everything is in place. Keely will not have to think about regular school until after the Olympics in two years. She will have two years of intense gymnastic training. And if all goes as we hope, a berth on the Olympic team. It can be done."

"You mean Keely will be leaving high school that soon?" Keely's mom groaned. She reached over and grasped Keely's arm. "Honey, what do you think of all this?"

"It's okay, Mom," Keely said. "I guess it has to be." Keely felt like Wassily was a steamroller and she was stuck in cement. She felt powerless to stop his momentum, even if she wanted to.

"You won't mind missing all those boring history and English classes, am I right?" Keely's dad asked with a happy smile. "You won't miss taking all those notes and being stuck in class having to take tests on stuff that doesn't mean anything to a girl like you. A girl who isn't a big brain like her brother."

"Yeah," Keely said. She had an empty feeling in the pit of her stomach. She had known it was in the cards for her to leave

West Bluff. She had known it now for a long time, and she had succumbed to the idea. But now that it was actually happening, she felt empty.

And she felt a little sad and sick.

7

"I can't believe you're really quitting school," Merriann wailed at lunch on Monday. Her eyes were wet.

She and Keely had been best friends since they were little kids. Keely knew it would seem so strange not to see each other regularly anymore. They had always followed each other in and out of every fad. They always liked the same music and insisted on buying the hot new clothes. Keely and Merriann had haunted the toy stores—then they hit the clothing stores as they grew.

"I have to do it," Keely said, fighting back her own tears.

"I suppose I'll never get to see you anymore," Merriann said.

"Sure you will. We can still meet and hang out," Keely said.

"When? You'll always be practicing at the gym!" Merriann said. "When you're not there, you'll be too tired to want to do anything. Besides, Addy and Liza are your best friends now. You hang out with them more than you do with me because you're all gymnasts. I don't even feel like I know you anymore."

"Oh, Merriann! It's only going to be until the Olympics. Then life will be normal again," Keely said.

"That's two whole years!" Merriann exclaimed. "By that time we'll be total strangers! High school will be almost over. If you win one of those stupid medals, you won't want anything to do with your old friends, anyway. You'll be riding in parades and waving to people and doing TV commercials."

"Merri, you could come to the Games and share in the excitement," Keely said. "It would be fun!"

Merriann threw the wrapper from her sandwich into a trash container. "I want us to be just regular freshmen, going to football rallies and talking about guys and stuff," she said. "I want us to shop at the mall and laugh ourselves sick. Oh, Keely!"

Keely grabbed her friend for a long hug before they had to go to separate classes.

All day Keely felt empty, realizing that this was, indeed, her last week in high school. The last time she'd go to the cafeteria and complain about the dry chicken and the lumpy mashed potatoes.

The last week to hear Ms. LaRue speaking poetry in her bad French accent. The last week for hitting the mad rush to the lockers and climbing over bodies to get at her algebra or biology book.

Keely kept telling herself how much she wanted that gold medal. It was a chance that would never come again. It might be her only chance in her whole life to do something extraordinary. If she didn't go for it now, the parade would pass her by.

It wasn't like in the antiquated days when women in their mid-twenties won the medals. Little girls ruled now. Little girls in pigtails who weighed almost nothing.

* * *

On Wednesday, Keely and Julio had lunch together.

"You look terrible," Julio said.

"You're just saying that because you're mad that I'm leaving school," Keely countered.

"I'm not happy about that, all right, but that's not why I'm saying you look terrible," Julio said. "You really don't look good. Look at how you're not even eating now."

"The meatloaf is terrible. It tastes like cardboard," Keely said.

"No, it's actually pretty good today. They put a lot of onion in it, and the catsup is good and hot. It's pretty good meatloaf, and you're just nibbling on the edge of it like a mouse," Julio said.

"Onions give me a stomachache," Keely said.

"Come on, Keely, you're not fooling me," said Julio. "You're eating like a bird to stay tiny for gymnastics. You're turning into a bag of bones."

"Julio, it's not good to be fat. Sure, I have to be slim to be a gymnast, but I don't want to be a fat girl anyway," Keely said.

"You'd never be fat. It's that gymnastic thing. Every time I see you, you look worse. I bet you don't weigh more than 90 pounds now," Julio said.

Keely had been avoiding food as much as possible. When she made a mistake and ate too much, she would compensate by throwing up. Last night when she weighed herself, Keely was down to 94 pounds, a pound less than even Wassily had asked her to be. She had felt such a sense of accomplishment when she saw that 94.

"No, I weigh more than 90," Keely said.

"What's the matter with your parents?" Julio demanded. "Don't they see how you look?"

"Julio, you're just letting your feelings run away with you," Keely said. "I'm fine, okay?"

Lately, Keely had been having a lot of headaches, but she took care of them with over-the-counter pills. Other than that, she felt all right. She wasn't even very hungry anymore. She was using Sandra Ashton's advice, and it was working. Just the thought of food seemed to make Keely sick.

When Friday came, Keely's friends at school threw a party for her over at a little pizza place down the street from the school. Julio came, but he still seemed angry and frustrated as Keely opened the silly gifts her friends brought.

After the party was over, Keely and Julio walked back to the school alone. Keely said, "I'm sorry, Julio. I didn't want to hurt you. That's the last thing I wanted to do. We can still be friends and see each other. I'm not leaving town or anything."

Julio turned his back. "That'll come next," he muttered. "Old Wassily will say you have to go off to a bigger city with him to get better competition."

"Julio, why don't you just wish me luck and support me?" Keely asked.

Julio looked at Keely now. "I know you like this stuff, this gymnastics, and I want you to be happy, but . . ." His voice trailed, and then he turned abruptly and walked away.

Now there was nothing left to do but finish cleaning out her locker and wait for her mom to pick her up.

When her mom came, Keely ran and jumped in the van.

"Are you okay, Keely?" her mom asked. "Have you been crying?"

"Maybe," Keely said, wiping her eyes.

"I'm sorry," Mrs. Wayne said. "I sure hope we're doing the right thing. I'm not all that gung ho about it, you know."

Keely cried harder as West Bluff High School moved out of sight. She didn't want to be leaving her school, her friends, Julio. She didn't want it to come to this. She thought she could have it all—the gymnastics, the shot at the gold medal, and her school and friends too.

At this moment, gymnastics left her cold, and even bitter.

* * *

When Keely arrived at the gym on Monday, Wassily Karpov greeted her with a smile on his face.

"You look absolutely perfect, Keely. You have been watching your weight, and now you are enchanting!" he said.

Keely smiled too. "Yeah, I'm down to 94 pounds," she said proudly.

"Come," Wassily said, leading her to a full-length mirror in the gym. "Can you see the difference? No more pudgy thighs. No more love handles. How sleek you look. Like a fine little racehorse. I can see you delighting the judges. 'The little sylph' they will call you. Yes! You will be a phenomenon."

Keely had weighed herself Monday morning right after she got up. She weighed less than she had weighed in two years. She told Wassily she weighed 94 pounds, but she actually weighed 89. She wanted to give herself a little space to fluctuate. She was so excited that she could hardly believe it when the needle had stopped at 89.

When her mom had put out bacon, eggs, and oatmeal that morning, Keely pretended to be eating. But she had only swallowed a cup of black coffee, one segment of grapefruit, and some vitamins. She weighed herself again then. She was still 89. Her diligence had paid off. She was finally feeling like she was in control.

Keely spent most of Monday practicing on the beam. She needed to work on her acrobatic series. It was required that she include at least two flight elements. And those had been rather weak at the invitational. Although she had worked hard, she was still a bit hesitant on the beam.

But there was a spotter, a young man who steadied the gymnasts as they worked on the beam. His name was Yuri, and he was Wassily's nephew. He had been working at Wassily's gym for a few months. Yuri had dark hair and intense black eyes.

Keely lay flat on the beam, reached back, and grasped it with both hands. Then she swung her legs overhead.

"Good!" Wassily shouted.

When Keely began practicing jumps and springs on the beam, Yuri stood by.

"Balance on your toes," Wassily said. "Stretch your legs as you swing the arms up . . . now, jump! Keep your eyes on the beam!" A note of distress came into Wassily's voice.

Keely began to fall toward the floor, but Yuri's strong hands caught her and steadied her.

"Ohhhh," Keely groaned.

"That was stupid," Wassily scolded, "stupid, stupid! That was a beginner's mistake. You are like a girl who is six years old and doesn't know anything. If you continue to be so stupid, you will never make it! It is a joke to send someone so clumsy to the Olympics!"

Tears pressed behind Keely's eyes. Why was he being so mean? She had gotten so tiny for him. She was trying her best. Did he have to be so cruel?

"Do it again, and this time do it right," Wassily said.

Keely was now thoroughly frightened of falling again. But Wassily had told the girls that fear was their worst enemy. You could not be afraid or you were lost. All the great ones knew no fear. That's what Wassily said. They ignored pain and they knew no fear. And they were all slim, lovely sylphs . . .

Keely was on the beam again. She had bruises on the balls of her feet and her heels. She had a blood blister on her big toe. Bouncing up and down on the beam with her feet was like torture. But she continued to do it with Wassily standing there glowering at her.

"Eyes on the beam every minute," Wassily instructed. "Keep your arms elevated to shoulder height. Spring into the air—gracefully! Gracefully! No, no, no, not like that! You fool. Have you any idea how clumsy you look?"

Tears streamed down Keely's face. She was shaking with sobs now.

"Crybaby, silly crybaby," Wassily ridiculed. "Go to the bathroom and wash your face. I will maybe get you a dolly to hold. You are a crybaby and crybabies need dollies. Go on, wash your face. Get out of my sight!"

Keely fled to the bathroom, choking with sobs.

8

"I m—made a terrible mistake," Keely cried to her mother when she came to pick Keely up. "I never should've quit school. Everything was so awful today. Wassily was so mean to me. I'm no good. I'll never get to the Olympics!"

"Now, Keely, you know that whatever you do, I'll be behind you. But you seemed pretty sure this was what you wanted," said Mrs. Wayne. "Don't let just one bad day discourage you that much."

"Oh, M—mom, I almost fell off the beam, and Wassily called me names when I cried. He said I was a crybaby. It was so awful," Keely said.

"I suppose that's the technique he uses to toughen the gymnasts," Keely's mom said. "It's his way of chastening you. Why don't we stop and get something to eat? I bet you haven't had time to eat all day. You must be starved."

"Yeah, I'm hungry," Keely said. "I want a sub sandwich. A turkey sub with everything on it. And a soda."

What difference did it make anyway? Keely thought. She was starving herself only to be abused by that cruel monster at the gym.

Keely wolfed down a six-inch sub sandwich with soda. She was almost frightened by how stuffed she felt. She was not used to feeling so satiated. Her stomach hurt.

As she thought more and more about what she had done, she became more distraught. She had probably added two or three pounds! Tomorrow Wassily's eagle eye would notice it the minute she put on her leotard. He would not only abuse her for her lack of skill on the beam, but he would ridicule her weight as well.

When Keely got home, she rushed to the bathroom. She turned on the faucet in the sink and flushed the toilet to make as much noise as possible. Then she stuck her finger down her throat. In a few seconds, she was vomiting.

Keely rinsed out her mouth and sprayed the bathroom with air freshener until the smell was gone. She flushed the toilet again. Then she sank to the floor, exhausted and depressed.

Keely thought that her mom must have said something to her dad. Because as Keely sat in the den looking at a home-study assignment, he came in and sat down beside her.

"How's it going, Princess?" her dad asked. "Today was a little rough, I understand." He didn't usually call Keely *Princess*, and he rarely sat down to talk to her, just the two of them. He even had a sympathetic look on his face.

"It was hard today, Dad," Keely said. "Wassily was really mean." She had a severe headache, and she was dizzy.

"Well, I suppose it's a little like boot camp. They make it pretty rough in the beginning to separate the men from the boys," her dad said.

"I was trying my best, Dad, but he kept screaming at me," Keely said, her lips quivering as tears threatened again.

"Listen, Keely," said Mr. Wayne. "I'm here to tell you that you can take anything that he throws at you. You're a Wayne. There's not a quitter bone in our bodies. No way. Tomorrow you are going back to that gym with your head held high, and you are going to master the beam and anything else Wassily deals. Because that's the kind of girl you are. *Resilient* is your middle name."

Keely looked at her father, half in admiration and half in fear. Her grandfather had been a poor black sharecropper with 11 children, and somehow he sent them all to college, including Keely's dad. All those children were success stories.

When Keely's dad was small, he had been part of the migrant worker pattern, picking berries throughout the South and Midwest. They would start in Florida in January. Then up through Louisiana and Arkansas. Then to Missouri, and up to Michigan for the strawberries. With impossible hard work and determination, they saved and scrimped—and won.

"Don't think I didn't feel like quitting a lot of times," Keely's dad often said. "But succeeding is the best revenge."

Now Mr. Wayne smiled at his daughter and said, "Two years from now when you are standing there with the whole world watching and they are putting that gold medal around your neck, Princess, then Wassily will have to admit you were the best he ever saw."

"I'll try," Keely said. But she felt weak, and her head hurt and her feet hurt. She hurt all over.

"You won't *try*. To say that is to admit you might not succeed. You will *win*. You will conquer the beam and everything else. Am I right?" her dad asked.

"Yeah," Keely whispered.

That night Keely had another nightmare. She was doing exercises on the beam, only this time the beam was 50 feet off the floor, not 4. When Keely stood on it and looked down, she saw Wassily, Yuri, and the other gymnasts as tiny figures. She stretched out her arms and began jumping.

Keely heard screams. She was falling . . . falling . . . She crashed to the floor below. All the faces crowded around her, shocked and saddened now. Keely was severely injured. She felt broken, broken all over. She heard someone say, "She will never walk again . . . she will never walk again . . . and she's so young . . ."

And then her dad's face loomed over her. "You will get up," he said. "You will get up right now because you are not hurt. You will get back on the beam, Keely, because that's the kind of girl you are."

Wassily said, "You clumsy, stupid girl. See what you have done now, Keely? You have ruined everything. They will blame me. I am ruined because they will all blame me. Oh—you—you have ruined me!"

Only Keely's mom was crying. Nobody but her mom. Even Addy and Liza did not look very sad. Maybe they even looked happy. Keely was competition for them. Now they had a better chance to get ahead.

Keely began to tremble, and she woke herself up with her sobs.

Relief flooded her. It was all a terrible nightmare. She had not fallen off the ridiculously high beam after all. She was in her own bed, and her back wasn't broken. Only her head ached, and she felt weak, and her big toe throbbed. But at least she didn't have a broken back.

Keely got out of bed, now thoroughly awake. She slid her feet into her slippers and went to the bathroom. She couldn't resist weighing herself. She looked down at the black numbers with trepidation. Ninety pounds. She had gained a pound. How did that happen? But it wasn't serious. She still weighed just 90 pounds. She was still—what did Wassily call her—the little sylph!

Keely opened the front door and went outside. The cool, fresh air felt so good. The sky was clear and filled with brilliant points of light—stars and planets. It had been a long time since Keely had seen the night sky at this hour.

Then, out of the darkness, a person appeared.

At first Keely was frightened. But then she saw who it was.

"Sandra!" Keely called out. Sandra Ashton was running past the house. At this hour! After midnight!

Sandra stopped but kept on jogging in place. "Hi, Keely, what are you doing outside in your PJs?"

"Just getting some fresh air," Keely said. "I heard you were in the hospital, Sandra. Are you better now?"

Sandra came a little closer. What Keely saw shocked her. Sandra wore a tank top and running shorts. Her arms were like sticks. Her legs had no curves to them. "Yeah, I was just a little run-down. I'm much better," Sandra said.

Sandra's beautiful face was bony, almost like a skeleton with skin stretched over it. She jogged in place a moment longer, then hurried on.

Poor Sandra, Keely thought. Something *must* be terribly wrong with her. She must have some wasting disease. A few years ago an old lady on the street had wasted away like that. She had become very emaciated, like Sandra. They said it was cancer.

Keely wondered if Reverend Paxton knew how sick Sandra was. They ought to be praying for her at church. Poor Sandra. She was so young and pretty, and she had such big dreams. What on earth could have stricken her like that?

When Keely went back inside, she realized she was very hungry. Years earlier, before she got serious about gymnastics, she'd sometimes get up in the middle of the night and get something to eat. Maybe a bagel with cream cheese or a cold cut sandwich from cold cuts in the fridge.

Keely used to love peeking into the refrigerator to see what tempted her. Now it was sort of like an enemy. The big white monster sheltering all those globs of fat.

But still, Keely was so hungry that she peered in.

Then she heard footsteps. Suddenly there was her dad, looking at her reproachfully. "Uh oh. The midnight raids on the fridge again," he scolded. "An attack of the munchies. I don't think so, Keely. You better just go back to bed."

"I was only going to get a peach or something," Keely said. Her hunger pangs were intense now. She knew she couldn't go to sleep if she didn't eat something. All she had eaten that day was some grapefruit, black coffee, and vitamins. Except for the sub sandwich she threw up.

"Keely, now isn't the time to return to the little pudge you were in middle school," her dad said.

"I was never fat. I only weighed 110 pounds," Keely said resentfully. He just didn't get it, Keely thought. He didn't understand what it was like to be a girl. He didn't understand what happened to girls' bodies once they began growing up. And of course, she was not going to try to explain it to him.

"On your small frame, 110 pounds is fat," her dad continued. "I'm sorry, but it is. Now go back to bed, okay?"

A feeling of desperation came to Keely. "I just need a peach or something," she said.

"You've eaten like a horse today," argued her dad. "You had a big breakfast, and Mom said you had a sub sandwich. Probably polished off a few cheeseburgers too. Come on, Keely. We're almost there. Let's not screw up now." His voice was now edged with annoyance.

Keely went back to bed, seething with resentment. She lay there and waited for her father to go back to her parents' bedroom. Then she got out of bed and sprinted back to the kitchen in her bare feet. She didn't even stop to put on her slippers.

Keely opened the refrigerator. There was a chocolate cake sitting on a plate under a lid. Keely yanked it out. Then, like a wild animal dragging food back to its lair, she carried the cake to her bedroom.

Keely sat in a chair, pulling off hunks of the cake and stuffing them into her mouth. She got the rich, gooey, dark frosting all over her face. She ran back to the kitchen and got a carton of milk, washing down the cake.

When she was finished, Keely had eaten the entire cake.

9

Keely didn't even have to stick her finger down her throat to vomit. She was sick for an hour, throwing up and feeling awful. Finally her mom rapped on the bathroom door. "You okay, baby?" she asked.

Keely quickly sprayed room freshener around the bathroom and opened the door. "Something I ate made me sick, Mom," she said. "Must've been that sub. But I'm okay now."

"My goodness, it's 2:00 in the morning, Keely," her mom said. "You have to get up early to go to the gym."

"Yeah, I'm okay now," Keely said, thankful that she had washed the frosting off her face before her mother saw her. When her mom had returned to the bedroom, Keely washed the cake plate. She hoped nobody remembered the chocolate cake tomorrow.

Keely lay awake in bed for a long time. The cake had been so good. She remembered what Liza had said. You could have anything you wanted as long as you took care of it before it made you fat.

Things were a little better in gymnastics class the next day when Keely started working on the beam again. She was more comfortable on it. Addy and Liza were there. School was out because of a teacher in-service day. So they were getting their turns being yelled at by Wassily. Wassily kept throwing it up to Addy how far down she had finished at the invitational.

When Keely took a break, Yuri came over. He was eating a nutrition bar. "You hungry?" he asked Keely. "I got plenty of these."

"No," Keely lied. She hated nutrition bars anyway. They tasted like sawdust to her.

"You are pretty skinny, Keely," Yuri said. "I never see you eating anything."

"Oh, I eat a lot. My mom makes these big meals. I always have a good breakfast. I guess that's the most important meal," Keely said, the lies coming more and more easily. Since she had begun trying to be thin, she lied all the time. To her family, to her friends, even sometimes to herself. Maybe all the time to herself. And sometimes she got all mixed up in the lies.

"You really want to get to the Olympics, huh?" Yuri asked.

"Yeah. I've got practically every book that was ever written about gymnastics," said Keely. "I've got books on Rigby and Retton and the American team that won the gold with Kerri Strug, and lots of others too. I've always idolized famous gymnasts."

"Well, you've got a lot of determination," Yuri said. "You gave up your regular life for a while, huh?" He seemed to be thinking hard about something. He seemed to be trying to decide if he should say something or not.

Finally Yuri looked directly at Keely and said candidly, "You know, it's probably none of my business. But I think you've got an eating problem."

"What?" Keely cried, frightened by his insight. "Yuri, that's so ridiculous. I eat good, healthy food. Fish, chicken, veggies, fruit, everything like that. I'm like the last person on earth with an eating problem."

"Yeah, maybe," Yuri said, sounding unconvinced. "But I've seen you around for several months now. And I know you weigh a lot less than you did when I first met you."

"Wassily said I needed to lose some weight, and so I did. I think I look much better now," Keely said. She was terrified that her secret would be uncovered and somehow it would get back to her parents that she had some eating disorder. Then everything would be ruined.

"Come on, Keely, weigh yourself," Yuri urged.

"I don't have to," said Keely defiantly. "I weighed myself this morning, and I weigh 95 pounds. Just what Wassily says I should weigh."

"Let's see if that's what the scales say," Yuri pressed.

"Yuri, are you calling me a liar or what?" Keely stormed. "I told you I weigh 95 pounds."

"You weigh 90 pounds—tops. Maybe less," Yuri said. "You'd better watch yourself, Keely. I'm not kidding you. You ever heard of Christy Henrich? She was a gymnast in the 1980s. She was very good, but she pushed herself too hard. Then somebody told her she was fat. So she starved herself. She got down to forty-some pounds, and eventually she died. She was only 22. You've got to be careful. I mean it."

Keely was shaken. She walked away from Yuri without saying a word.

As Keely practiced jump mounts to the beam, Wassily seemed pleased. He even praised her, and her spirits rose. At the end of the day, Keely was exhausted but happy with herself.

Keely was catching a ride home with Addy. They planned to stop off at the food court at the mall for something to eat.

"What do you feel like?" Addy asked as the girls walked into the food court.

"A big cheeseburger," Keely said.

Addy turned and stared at Keely. "You sure? I thought you'd want some skimpy salad."

"No, it's okay. I'm down to 90 pounds. I can afford to eat a cheeseburger once in a while," Keely said.

"Wow! You *are* thin," Addy said, envy in her eyes.

Keely ordered a cheeseburger and a chocolate shake. Addy just got some chicken strips and ice water. But midway through the cheeseburger, Keely got sick. She ran to the bathroom. She was sick to her stomach and disoriented for a few minutes as everything went out of her.

"My body is getting crazy," Keely complained when the girls were back in the car. "It's turning on me, Addy!"

"Keely," Addy said suddenly, "what if, after all this, we don't make it?"

"You mean the Olympics?" Keely asked.

"Yeah. What if we're not good enough?" Addy asked.

"Dad said you can't have negative thoughts, or it'll happen," Keely said.

"But how many girls in the whole world get to the Olympics?" Addy asked. "You can count on the fingers of two hands American girls who've gotten gold."

"You're not thinking of quitting, are you, Addy?" Keely asked after a silent pause.

"I don't know," said Addy. "I don't want to quit high school like you did and Wassily says I have to. My parents want me to go for it. 'Go for the gold,' they say. But . . . I don't know. My heart's not in it anymore. Not like it used to be . . ."

All evening after she got home, Addy's words haunted Keely. What if Addy was right? What if neither of them got a place on the Olympic team? Only six girls qualified every Olympics. Maybe, Keely thought, she didn't have the right stuff to push herself for the next two years either . . .

"You look like you're worried about something, honey," Keely's mom said after dinner.

"No, I'm fine," Keely said. She couldn't bring herself to share her doubts with her mom. She knew her mom would support her, but she would tell Keely's dad. They shared everything. And her dad would be angry and brokenhearted.

"Did practice go better today, Keely?" her mom asked.

"Yeah, much better," said Keely. "Wassily even praised me a couple of times."

"You see? Didn't I tell you not to let one bad day discourage you?" Keely's mom said, smiling.

* * *

Thursday after practice Keely heard a lot of horns honking. She stepped outside into the cool evening. A pair of cars with kids from West Bluff High School were driving down the street, sounding their horns and screaming. The cheerleaders were waving their pom-poms from the side windows.

"What's going on, you guys?" Keely shouted as the first car slowed down.

"We're having a pep rally, Keely," Merriann shouted. "The big game is Friday. We're going against Jefferson. It's the biggest game of the year. Come on, jump in. We're all going to my house for pizza. Can't you come, just for a little while?"

Keely wanted to go, but she had to get to bed early. She ached all over from today's work. Her big toe was swollen, and the soles of her feet hurt something fierce. She was almost swimming in Ben-Gay, and she had her usual headache. Keely needed to recover. Wassily said that he wanted Keely in 'Olympic form' on the beam tomorrow. He was expecting an unblemished performance.

"I'd like to come, Merriann, but I just can't," Keely said, sadly. "You guys have a good time."

Merriann waved, and the cars full of teenagers rolled on down the street. Keely stood there, suddenly aware of how alone she felt. She would probably never attend another high school football game again as a teenager. She'd miss all the excitement. And she wouldn't go to any high school dances. She'd miss the junior-senior prom. She'd miss the homecoming balls. She wouldn't go with her friends to grill out on the beach. She wouldn't be in the West Bluff swing choir anymore. She probably would even have to quit the church choir pretty soon.

All she would have left was gymnastics.

And she was scared that it wasn't enough.

There were so many fascinating books written about young girls who won medals in the Olympics. They were the paragons of the sport. It all looked so wonderful. But, Keely thought, there weren't any books about the girls who sacrificed their teen years trying and never made the grade. How did they feel? There should be books about the losers, Keely thought. Little skinny girls who gave up their lives chasing a dream that never came true. Little waifs who struggled with sore toes and aching feet, who didn't even rate a footnote in a book.

Then Keely remembered what Yuri had said.

She thought about that girl he had mentioned, Christy Henrich.

Keely looked in her gymnastics books, but there was nothing there about Christy. Keely looked in 12 books before she finally found something about Christy.

She read that Christy finished fifth at the National Junior Championships when she was 14. She finished tenth in the All-Around competition at the Senior Nationals when she was 16. She seemed to have a good shot at the Olympics.

Christy missed getting a berth in the 1988 Olympics by 0.118 of a point in a vault in the compulsories. So she never got to the Games. But by that time, she had such a severe eating disorder that she couldn't fight her way back to health.

Keely felt hungry. She went to the kitchen. She wondered what the gang was doing at Merriann's. Probably stuffing themselves with pizza and chips. That's what they usually did. Julio was probably making jokes with Tanya Stone, that quiet girl he talked to sometimes. Julio was probably on the way to forgetting all about Keely . . .

Keely stood before the refrigerator, resentment boiling up inside her. She felt like she might explode with the hurt.

10

Keely found a bagel and spread on cream cheese thickly. Then she wolfed it down with gulps of milk, keeping an eye on the door. She heard her parents laughing in the living room, watching some sitcom on television.

Keely walked through the house to the bathroom. It was a familiar ritual now—her covert operation. It didn't even disgust her like it once had. It was something almost natural. Something you did after you ate, like brushing your teeth.

Keely hung over the toilet for a minute, but then she didn't stick her finger down her throat. Instead, she went to the den. She took down a book on health. She looked up "eating disorders."

"Bulimia," she read. "A binge-purge syndrome where food is consumed in a short span of time and then purged by vomiting, laxatives, or excessive exercise."

Keely trembled, but she continued reading.

She learned that sometimes bringing up food in forced vomiting rots your teeth. The stomach acid damages the enamel on the teeth. Sometimes your throat gets swollen, and even your fingernails rot from swimming in stomach acid.

Keely went to her bedroom and stepped on the scales then. She weighed 87 pounds.

Keely cried herself to sleep. But she didn't sleep long. The wail of an ambulance woke her up around midnight. At first, she incorporated the sound into her dream. But then she realized it was real. It was on her street.

Keely pulled on a robe and slid into slippers before going out to the living room. Her parents stood at the open door.

"Where's it stopped?" Keely asked.

"In the cul-de-sac," her dad answered. "Must be poor old Mr. Peterson having one of his heart spells."

Only the paramedics didn't go into the Petersons' house. They hurried into the house next door where the Ashtons lived.

"I wonder what's wrong there," Keely's mom said.

Keely came closer to her parents. "Sandra has been sick. I saw her the other night, and she looked terrible. She looked like she has some horrible disease."

Both Keely's parents turned and stared at her.

"Sandra is only a young girl," Keely's dad said. "And I haven't heard anything about a disease. I played golf with her father last Saturday. I'm sure he would've mentioned it."

"I just had lunch with Martina Ashton," Keely's mom said. "That was last Wednesday. She said Sandra was doing fine, just working a little too hard."

The Waynes walked down the street toward the Ashton house. They wanted to see if there was anything they could do.

When Keely's mom saw Mrs. Ashton, she ran and hugged her. "Oh, Marti, what happened?" she asked.

"Sandra collapsed . . . from exhaustion, I think," said Sandra's mom. "She's been working so hard on her dance routines. She's just a bit overwrought. The big audition is coming up." A ghost of a smile flickered on the woman's face. "I'm sure she'll be fine."

Mrs. Ashton rode off in the ambulance with Sandra. Mr. Ashton followed in the car. Then the Waynes started home.

"Did you guys see Sandra on the gurney?" Keely asked.

"She's so pale," her dad said.

"And thin," her mom said with a shudder.

"She almost looked like she was dead," Keely said.

Keely's mom turned sharply toward her. "What an awful thing to say!" she yelled, obviously shaken.

In the morning, Keely ate a little oatmeal and drank her orange juice. She hadn't slept all night. She had done a lot of thinking about what she had read about eating disorders—and Sandra. Pieces were starting to fit together in her head.

Keely was going to catch a ride from Addy to practice. But Keely had decided she didn't want to go to the gym. "Addy, just drop me off at Levitt Hospital. I'll take the bus home," she said after jumping in the car.

"Keely! You're cutting gymnastics? Wassily will kill you!" Addy cried. "This is a really important practice!"

"Just drop me off," Keely said quietly as she watched the scenery blur by the side window.

Keely walked into the lobby of the large hospital and asked what room Sandra Ashton was in. She was told that Sandra was in intensive care and couldn't have any visitors but close family.

Keely then went to the intensive care waiting room. She saw Mr. Ashton sitting in one of the cold, leatherlike chairs. The Ashtons had both had brief careers in show business before settling into different careers. They were attractive, talented people.

Sandra had begun dancing as a small child. She appeared in the *Nutcracker* and *Babes in Toyland* shows locally every holiday season. She had even been on a television special.

"Mr. Ashton," Keely asked, "how is Sandra?"

The man looked very drawn. "Oh, Keely . . . how nice of you to come," he said quietly. "My wife is with her now. She . . . Sandra . . . she's a very sick girl. We are in a state of shock. It seems, unbelievably, that she is dangerously undernourished."

Keely remembered what she had read the night before about bulimia and anorexia.

"I'm afraid our daughter reduced her weight in a way that was out of control," Mr. Ashton said.

"I hope she's better soon," Keely said.

"Oh yes, I'm sure she will be," Mr. Ashton said. "And thanks again for coming. When she's out of intensive care, we'll let you know."

But Keely never got to see Sandra.

After three days in the hospital, Sandra still had not come out of the coma she had fallen into. Mrs. Ashton had called Keely's mom in tears on the fourth day with the prognosis. "Oh, Jill, we're losing her!" she cried.

Keely's mom had tried to console Mrs. Ashton. But when she hung up the phone, she looked wide-eyed at Keely and asked, "Would you believe that Sandra is near death because she's been starving herself to stay thin?"

"Yes," Keely said in a very small voice. "I'm doing the same thing."

"What?" her mom gasped. Her eyes instantly filled with tears.

Once Keely started talking, she couldn't stop, emptying herself of her awful secrets.

"I'm starving myself and making myself throw up and stuff," she said. "I only weigh 86 pounds now. My throat hurts, and I've got a headache all the time." Keely started sobbing.

"Oh, my God," Keely's mom said, rushing to Keely. She put her arms around her, as if she could protect her from the damage that had already been done. "How did I not know? How could I have not seen it?"

"It's not your fault," said Keely in between sobs.

"We'll get through this, sweetie," cooed her mom as she rocked her daughter back and forth. "We'll do what it takes. We'll make it right together."

"But what about Dad?" Keely whispered. She had been almost afraid to ask. "What if I decide to quit gymnastics? I'll let him down. He'll never forgive me. He'll disown me."

"Don't worry about your dad," Keely's mom said with strength Keely didn't know she had. "You worry about yourself. He'll have to deal with it. And honey, if he can't deal with it, just remember that it's *his* problem, not yours. It's your body and your life."

Keely's mom continued to hold her daughter as they both shed mixed tears of sorrow, relief, and fear.

* * *

Keely quit gymnastics the day after Sandra Ashton died of liver and kidney failure. The doctors said she was so malnourished that her organs just shut down.

Keely brought one perfect red rose to put on Sandra's coffin. There were so many flowers, but Keely felt sure that somehow Sandra knew about the perfect red rose.

Then Keely turned, her shoulders straight and her jaw set. She had made a decision. She was returning to West Bluff High School. She was going to recover her teenaged life.

And that would be gold enough for any girl.

PASSAGES Novels by Anne Schraff

The Boy from Planet Nowhere
Gingerbread Heart
The Hyena Laughs at Night
Just Another Name for Lonely
Memories Are Forever
The Power of the Rose
The Shining Mark
Summer of Shame
To Slay the Dragon